A PACK OF Wolf TALES

retold by **Ann Jungman**
illustrated by **Vicki Yeates**

CONTENTS

LONGMAN

PETER AND THE WOLF

(RUSSIA)

Long ago and far away in Russia, near to a great
forest, lived Peter with his grandfather.
Grandfather's house was cosy. It sat in the
middle of a pretty garden surrounded by a high
wall. Inset in the wall was a stout wooden gate.

"We need that big wall to keep the wolves out,"

Grandfather told Peter, "and if you go out, don't go far and always remember to shut the gate. We don't want that cunning Mr Wolf to sneak in when we're not looking."

"Of course, Grandfather," said Peter, nodding seriously.

Outside the garden, just beyond the gate was a pond, beside which was a large tree. Every day, Peter went out of the garden to feed bread to his great friend the duck who lived on the pond.

One day, Peter walked down the garden path, as usual, opened the gate, as usual, forgot to close the gate, as usual, and fed the duck, as usual.

High up in the branches of the tree sat a tiny bird. The bird was very hungry and was hoping to get a crumb of the bread that Peter was throwing to the duck. In fact, the bird was so very hungry that she decided to swoop down and snatch a bit of the bread. Hidden in some bushes close by, the cat was watching her...

The bird flew down and grabbed some bread in her beak. At the same moment the cat leapt up at the bird... and caught a tail feather in his paws.

"Shoo!" yelled Peter at the cat.

"Miaow!" howled the cat miserably.

"Tweet, tweet!" sang the bird.

"Quack, quack!" chorused the duck.

Hearing all this noise, Grandfather rushed down the path and saw the open gate.

"How many times have I told you never to leave this gate open? Come in this minute, Peter! I'm going to lock the gate till winter is over. How would you feel if a wolf got in? My blood freezes just to think about it." Grandfather took out a big key and locked the gate.

Later that evening, Grandfather's worst fears almost came true. A wolf crept out of the forest and stood by the gate and looked hungrily around. The bird flew up to a high branch, tweeting loudly to warn the cat. The cat climbed the tree as fast as he could.

Only the duck, swimming at the edge of the pond, was left where the wolf could catch her. She should have swum right into the middle of the pond, where she would have been safe, but

she panicked. Making a terrible noise, the duck tried to get out of the water. The wolf grabbed her and swallowed the poor duck whole.

The terrified cat and the bird, each on a different branch of the tree, looked on helplessly. They hoped the wolf would go away now that he had eaten the duck, but no such luck! The wolf was still hungry and thought he would enjoy a juicy snack of cat and bird. He couldn't climb the tree to get to them, but he circled round and round the tree, showing a mouthful of sharp pointed teeth.

The bird could have flown away, but the cat was trapped. The bird, who was full of daring and goodwill, decided to stay to comfort the cat. She flew down to sit on the same branch as the cat… but making sure that there was some distance between them.

Peter, inside the house, had heard the duck screeching and quacking followed by an ominous silence.

"Whatever is going on?" thought Peter and he rushed to his bedroom window just in time to see the duck disappear down the wolf's throat. A big tear ran down Peter's face – he had really loved the duck. Then he saw the cat and the bird cowering on the branch and the yellow-eyed snarling wolf below.

"I must help them," thought Peter. "That is what the duck would have wanted." He rushed outside, and grabbing a length of rope and a ladder, scaled the garden wall. He sat on top of the wall, just a short distance from the branch on which the bird and the cat were sitting.

The wolf saw Peter and leapt up to get at him, but the wall was a little too high for him to reach.

Meanwhile Peter whispered to the bird, "Fly around and attract the wolf's attention, but mind his sharp teeth."

The bird did as Peter said. While the wolf chased the bird, Peter made his rope into a lasso.

At just the right moment, the bird flew noisily up to Peter. With split-second timing Peter lowered the loop and the wolf put his head straight in.

"Got you!" shouted Peter triumphantly and pulled the rope tightly round the wolf's throat. The wolf let out a howl of rage and struggled to escape. That brought Grandfather rushing out.

At that very moment, two hunters ran out of the nearby forest. They had been tracking the wolf.

"Help me to tie up the wolf," cried Peter.

"Well done, my boy," said the hunters. "What a brave act!"

"Tweeeet!" sang the bird proudly.

"Miaow!" agreed the cat.

"Peter!" shouted Grandfather. "You disobeyed me, but I am glad. You have caught the wolf all by yourself. You make me very happy."

The hunters tied the wolf to a pole and carried him into town for everyone to see. Peter marched in front of the wolf with Grandfather and the cat and the bird behind. The townsfolk turned to cheer and wave. Suddenly, someone called out, "Quiet everyone, listen."

The cheering stopped and there was total silence. From inside the wolf's tummy came a weak "quack".

"Quick, kill the wolf and get my poor duck out," cried Peter.

At that, the hunters killed the wolf. The duck rejoined his friends and they had the biggest feast to celebrate that anyone could remember.

THE THREE LITTLE PIGS

(BRITAIN)

One day, three little pigs sat shivering together under a tree trying to shelter from the rain.

"I'm freezing," said the first little pig.

"I'm soaking wet," moaned the second little pig.

"What we need is a good strong house," declared the third little pig. "Then we would be fine and dry when it rains and when it is cold we could have a big log fire."

"What a good idea!" squeaked the first and second little pigs.

As soon as it stopped raining, the first little pig set off down the road to buy some materials to build a house. He soon met a man carrying a load of straw.

"Oh Mr Man, Mr Man, will you sell me your straw?" cried the little pig.

"And what would you want my straw for, little pig?"

"To build a fine house, Mr Man, to shelter from the rain and the cold."

"Five pounds for my straw," said the man. The little pig paid him the five pounds and set about building the house.

No sooner was the house finished than who should wander past but Mr Wolf. Seeing the first little pig looking out of the window, Mr Wolf smiled to himself and knocked on the front door.

"Let me in, little pig," he called.

"No, I will not let you in," cried the first little pig. He knew that Mr Wolf meant him no good. "By the hair on my chinny, chin, chin, I will not let you in."

"Then I'll huff and I'll puff and I'll blow your house down."

At that, Mr Wolf huffed and puffed. He blew down the house of straw, and ate the first little pig.

The next week, the second little pig set out to build a house. As he walked along, he met a man leading a cart filled with wood.

"Mr Man, Mr Man, please sell me your wood," said the little pig.

"And what would a little pig like you want with a pile of wood?" asked the man.

"I want to build a house, so that I can keep warm and dry," the little pig told him.

"Ten pounds for my wood," said the man, "Not a penny less."

So the second little pig bought the wood and

quickly built himself a very pretty house. No sooner had he finished than who should come walking down the road but that same Mr Wolf who had eaten the first pig. Mr Wolf grinned broadly when he saw the second little pig putting the finishing touches to his house.

"Good day to you, little pig," shouted Mr Wolf. "That's a very fine house you have there. May I come in and have a look?"

"Certainly not," cried the second little pig, running inside the house and slamming the front door. "I know what your game is, I'm not daft. By the hair on my chinny, chin, chin, I will not let you in," he shouted.

"Then I'll huff and I'll puff and I'll blow your house down," snarled mean Mr Wolf, and he huffed and he puffed and he puffed and he huffed until the wooden house finally fell down. By that time Mr Wolf was very hungry and angry and he ate the second little pig in two minutes flat.

Not long after, the third little pig set off to build a house. Walking along the road, he met a man with a big cart full of bricks.

"Mr Man, Mr Man, may I buy those bricks from you, please?"

"And what would a little pig like you want with all these bricks?"

"Please, Mr Man, I need to build a good strong house to keep me dry and warm and safe from Mr Wolf."

"The bricks are yours for twenty pounds," said the man.

"Done!" cried the little pig.

The third little pig worked very hard building his lovely brick house. He made some cement and carefully laid one brick on top of another. Then he built a roof with a big chimney pot. When it was finished, the little pig went outside to admire his handiwork.

"Wonderful!" he said, smiling to himself. "What

a splendid strong house I have built and it looks good too." Just then, he saw Mr Wolf ambling along the road towards him.

"Help!" cried the third little pig and he ran into his house and locked the door.

"Good day, young pig," called Mr Wolf, "What a splendid house you have built. Bricks are much better than straw or wood. May I come in and give you a lovely house-warming present?"

"No way!" shouted the third little pig. "I know you only want to eat me. By the hair on my chinny, chin, chin, I will not let you in."

"Then I'll huff and I'll puff and I'll blow your house down," screamed the angry Mr Wolf, but no matter how much he huffed and puffed, he simply could not blow down the house of bricks and mortar.

"I'll get you yet, little pig!" he shrieked, "One way or another, I'll get you! You won't escape from me so easily." He grabbed a ladder and

nipped up onto the pig's roof and began to climb down the chimney.

The third little pig panicked for a moment and then pushed a big cauldron of boiling water into the fireplace at the bottom of the chimney. Mr Wolf fell into the water with a splash and a howl and was turned into wolf soup. The little pig enjoyed the soup for several days and from then on lived happily ever after in his strong brick house.

A WOLF'S VERSION OF THE THREE LITTLE PIGS

(FROM LUCY AND THE BIG BAD WOLF)

So off went Gran and the mums, and 2.15 and the children stayed behind and had a lovely day together.★ After playing with them in the park and giving them their tea, 2.15 settled the children down in a small circle to listen to a story. He picked up a book.

★2.15 is a Wolf. He called himself 2.15 after the train to London on which he was travelling when he decided he needed a name.

'Alright, kids, this is your lucky day. Your Uncle 2.15 is going to read you a story.'

He glanced casually at the title of the book he had picked up. It was 'The Three Little Pigs'.

2.15 began to read the familiar story and the children joined in the chorus of 'I'll huff and I'll puff and I'll blow your house down.' When he finally finished the story 2.15 snapped the book shut.

'That,' he declared, 'that story was a load of old gubbins, and very unfair to wolves. I shall now tell you the true story of what really happened.

'Once upon a time there lived three fat, horrible, smelly pink pigs. They were so yukky and disgusting that you wouldn't have wanted to meet them, not even after they were turned into bacon. Well, one day these three revolting, utterly yukky little pigs were walking along the road when who should they be fortunate enough to meet but elegant and clever Mr Wolf.

' "Good morning, little pigs," said Mr Wolf, who had the most beautiful manners. "And where are you off to?"

' "We're going to town to buy some materials to build ourselves a house" squeaked the three smelly, disgusting and thoroughly yukky pigs.

'Now the wolf knew very well that the three pigs were lazy and ignorant and stupid, as well as fat and disgusting and thoroughly yukky, and he knew that if *he* didn't show them how to build their house, they would waste all their money and effort. So Mr Wolf, despite the fact that he was very busy and on his way to a party, decided to show these three utterly revolting little pigs how to build a proper house.

' "What will you build your house of?" asked Mr Wolf.

' "Straw," piped up the first little piggy-wig.

' "Alright," said the wolf (who as well as being

elegant and polite and clever, was also a very good teacher and knew that the only way to learn was from your mistakes). "Alright, you go and buy some straw and build a house."

'So the first horrid little pig went and wasted some money on straw to build a house with. And who was it who sold that silly little pig the straw? Why, a man of course. And did that man bother to tell the silly little pig that straw was no use to build a house with? No, he did not. Mr Wolf looked at the pile of straw.

' "Now you try and build the house," said Mr Wolf, knowing that the pig would have to learn from his experience. So he sat patiently while the first little pig built his big straw house.

'When it was finished the silly little pink piggy looked pleased with himself.

' "Now go inside and see if it's strong enough," instructed the wolf. And the silly piggy obediently went inside.

' "Right," said Mr Wolf, "I'll huff and I'll puff and I'll blow your house down."

'And he huffed and he puffed and blew the house down. The pig stood in the middle and looked in amazement at the fallen straw, and he began to cry.

' "Don't you worry", said kind Mr Wolf, lending him a handkerchief. "It was all a learning experience."

'So the first little pig cheered up, and went off

with the second little pig. They both went and bought some wood, and they built another house.

' "Will you huff and puff, please, Mr Wolf, and see if you can blow this one down," they called to Mr Wolf, who was going to be very late for his party. And kind Mr Wolf huffed and puffed as they had requested and, of course, down came their house. This time two little piggies were very upset.

' "Now, you just try and think what you can learn from this experience," said Mr Wolf.

' "I know," said the third little piggy. "Let's spend more money and build a brick house."

' "Now *that* is a good idea," said Mr Wolf. "I've got to hurry to get to my party. So here's some money towards the cost of the house, and on my way home I'll come this way, even though it's a long way round, and check that you've done everything right."

'So after having a wonderful time at the wolf party, Mr Wolf made a special detour to pass by the little pigs' house. It really looked like a proper house now.

' "Oh good," thought Mr Wolf. "Those three yukky and very silly pink pigs have got it right this time. I knew they would," and he knocked three times on the door. The three little pigs looked out of the window.

' "Hello Mr Wolf," they called, "Why don't you try to huff and puff and blow our house down."

'So poor, tired Mr Wolf stood in the road and called, "I'll huff and I'll puff and I'll *blow* your house down." And even though he had been dancing for hours, he huffed and puffed as hard as he could, but still the house stood.

' "You've done very well, little pigs," said Mr Wolf. "Now you'll be safe and sound."

' "But Mr Wolf," squeaked one of the little pigs,

"there's a slate loose on the roof. What shall we do about it?"

' "Well, that's no problem," said Mr Wolf. "Just put this ladder against the side of the house, climb up and put the slate back."

'So each of the three little pigs tried to climb up the ladder, but they were all too pink and fat to get very far. So kind Mr Wolf nipped up the ladder and fixed the slate. But those horrid and stupid little piggy-wigs took the ladder away while he was up there, and Mr Wolf had no choice but to climb down the chimney to get

down. While Mr Wolf was climbing down the chimney the absolutely beastly little piggies even tried to light a fire, but they were too silly to manage it. So yet again Mr Wolf came to the rescue. He showed those three stupid little pigs how to light a fire, and then every day he came to fetch the pigs and take them for a run until they got thin and fit and could nip up the ladder as quick as one, two, three. And that, children, is the end of the true story of Mr Wolf and the Three Yukky Little Pigs.

'I like the other version better,' grumbled Wayne.

'I liked 2.15's one better,' said Sharon and Karen. Darren and Stacey agreed.

'Course you do,' said 2.15. 'It's much better *and* more accurate!'

From *Lucy and the Big Bad Wolf* by Ann Jungman

WOLFSKIN'S BRIDE

(AN INUIT STORY, NORTHERN CANADA)

In the far, far north of Canada, in the icy lands, lived a man and his wife and daughter. At night they lay huddled in their igloo, and as often as not, they went to bed hungry. One morning in the middle of the long, cruel winter the daughter got up early and went out into the

thick snow. There, lying on the ground in front of her, lay a freshly killed caribou.

"Father," she called, "come quickly. Someone has left us a whole carcass of caribou."

"What foolishness are you talking, daughter?" snapped her father as he came out into the snow. Then he saw that she was telling the truth and his face burst into a smile.

"Now we can eat our fill and not be hungry for weeks," he said.

Her mother smiled broadly too. "What a blessing, daughter."

That night, the girl woke to see a tail disappearing through the door. "It's all very odd," she said to herself. "Somehow the meat and the visitor must be linked."

The next morning, there was a fine dead seal outside the igloo.

"Together with the caribou meat, this seal will keep us in food all winter," said her father

cheerfully. "What good luck we are having."

Once again, the girl woke in the middle of the night and felt a presence in the room.

"Who's there?" she called, jumping out of bed. There was no answer, but she saw a wolf tail disappear through the door. "It is as if a wolf is finding us food," thought the girl.

The following night, as the family were about to eat supper, a young man dressed in wolf skins walked into their igloo.

"Come," he said to the girl. "You are to be my bride."

The girl and her parents were shocked into silence.

Hardly a moment had passed when another young man, this time dressed in wolverine furs, strode into the room. He tried to grab the girl.

"You may have got here first," the newcomer shouted at the man in wolf skins, "but she is mine. I'm the one she will marry."

"I'll fight you for her," shouted Wolfskin.

"Outside!" insisted the father. "No fighting in here."

All night the, sound of a fierce battle could be heard.

"Don't go out," the father commanded his daughter. "This fight is none of our concern."

But the girl had fallen in love with Wolfskin and lay awake tossing and turning until the first signs of morning, when she got up and anxiously went out into the snow. Two sets of tracks led away from the igloo — a wolf's and a wolverine's — and the snow was stained with red blood. The girl was frightened but forced herself to follow the blood-stained trail. Eventually, she found the wolverine dead. When the girl told her father he said, "Forget it, daughter. This is not our business."

As they were eating their meal that evening, the door opened and in came an old man. He was dressed in a wolf skin.

"Your daughter must come at once," he said, "My son is dying. Only she can help."

At once the girl ran to put on her furs and left the igloo with the old man. As soon as they were well away from her parents' home, he said, "Quick, climb on my back."

The girl did as she was told and, although it was too dark to see, she felt as if she was riding on a wolf. Eventually, they reached a small hut. There

in a corner lay Wolfskin looking very pale and near to death.

"I have brought your bride. You need not die," cried the old man.

The girl knelt down and began to nurse Wolfskin with love and tenderness. As soon as he recovered, the two married and were happy together. Not long after, Wolfskin was well enough to go out and hunt again.

Every night he went out and every morning came back with fresh meat. The girl begged her husband to take her with him one night, but he always refused. Every night she lay in bed wondering what his secret was, but she loved him and they were a happy couple.

Then one day, Wolfskin heard that there was going to be a dance. "Let's go," he said to his wife. "It's time we had a little fun."

"No, don't!" cried the old man. "It would be dangerous. Someone wants to do you harm."

"Who?" cried Wolfskin's bride.

"My son was not the only one who loved you. The other died for you and his spirit walks and looks for revenge."

Wolfskin just laughed and they went to the dance and danced all night. The girl got so hot that she went outside for a moment to cool off in the snow. As she was rubbing some snow on her face, a little girl came running up to her and said, "Quick, quick, come, my grandmother needs you. Hurry, it's very important." She tugged at Wolfskin's bride's arm urgently. Reluctantly, the girl went with the child.

Eventually, they reached a cave. Inside, they found the child's grandmother stirring a big pot over the fire.

"Greetings to you," cried the old woman. "I thank you for coming. Now take off all your clothes and come here and let me wash you." The girl was uncomfortable, but didn't want to be rude, so she did as she was told. The child also took off her clothes. The grandmother then washed both of them with the contents of the pot.

Within an instant, Wolfskin's bride had shrunk to the size of the child and the child grew into a beautiful young woman. The young woman then grabbed the bride's clothes and ran to join Wolfskin.

Wolfskin's true bride followed her to Wolfskin's hut and knocked on the door. When Wolfskin answered she tried to explain what had happened, but he just laughed and said, "Go away, little girl. You're no bride of mine," and he put his arms round the false bride and disappeared into the house.

Wolfskin's bride was in despair and sat down in the snow and wept. Her sobbing was interrupted by another little girl who urged her to get up. "Come on, my grandmother wants you – no time to waste," she said.

"Why would I come with you," wept the true

bride, "when it's all because of a grandmother that I have shrunk to the size of a child and have lost my dear Wolfskin to another?"

"You must come, you must," insisted the child. "Please come, or you will lose Wolfskin forever."

This so frightened the unhappy girl that she went with the child.

"Enter," cried a kindly looking old woman, as she stirred a big cauldron. "Enter and take off your clothes and I will wash you from head to toe."

The girl did as she was told and suddenly realised that she was herself again. The old woman gave her a dress and said, "Go and find your husband and pour this liquid into the false bride's ear while she is asleep."

"Then what?" asked the girl.

"Continue to love your husband and live a good life," said the old woman.

The girl crept into her husband's hut and saw that he was asleep next to the false bride. She poured the liquid into the sleeping girl's ear and instantly the false bride turned into a child again. Wolfskin awoke and realised in a flash that the child was a witch and turned her out into the snow. When he came back into his hut, he held up a lamp and saw that it was truly his bride standing there.

"Forgive me," said Wolfskin, "I knew something was not right, but I didn't understand what. My father was right. The spirit of the wolverine is trying to spoil our happiness."

"My darling husband, my own Wolfskin, bad

spirits tried but they have not succeeded. Now let us enjoy each other and grow old together in harmony."

Wolfskin and his wife had many children and the whole family was well known for being content and kind. When they were very old, Wolfskin spoke to his wife.

"We have been very happy for many years, have we not?"

"Why yes, husband, how can you ask?"

"And in all those years did you not guess that I am not an ordinary man?"

"Of course," she replied. "In your spirit and sometimes in your body you are a wolf."

"And that knowledge has not worried you?"

"Why no!"

"I only became a human for love of you," he told her. "Now I want to return to my wolf life, but I do not want to leave you."

"Then we shall run together as wolves," said his wife.

So Wolfskin and his wife gathered their children around them.

"The time has come, my dear children," he said, "for us to depart for another land. Share everything we have equally among you and be as happy as we have been. Farewell, my precious ones."

They all embraced and kissed and wept.

Then Wolfskin and his wife went outside and knelt in the snow. After a few moments, they turned into wolves and ran off happily into the forest to continue their lives in a new and different way.

BRER WOLF TRIES TO CATCH BRER RABBIT

(USA)

One day, Brer Fox was walking down the road thinking about what he always thought about… how to catch Brer Rabbit. Brer Fox was

thinking so hard that he didn't notice Brer Wolf coming towards him and he went SLAP BLAM right into him.

"Hey, Cousin Fox," cried Brer Wolf, getting up off the road, "what is going on in your head? You walked straight into me!"

"Sorry, Cousin Wolf," replied Brer Fox. "Please excuse me, I was thinking so hard about how I could catch Brer Rabbit that I wasn't looking where I was going."

"You have been trying to catch Brer Rabbit for as long as I have known you, Cousin Fox, and that is a mighty long time," said Brer Wolf.

"Don't remind me!" groaned Brer Fox. "But that pesky rabbit always manages to find some sneaky way to escape from me. He's so clever and mischievous and cunning."

"I know it, I know it, Cousin Fox," exclaimed Brer Wolf, "and it's just not right that two creatures such as us, whom everyone fears, should be outwitted time and time again by a no-account creature like a rabbit."

"True, true," agreed Brer Fox, "but I've tried every trick I know to catch him and they never, never work."

"Well," said Brer Wolf importantly, "I have a brilliant plan but it will only work if we can persuade Brer Rabbit to come to your house."

"Huh, no chance of that," sniffed Brer Fox. "He wouldn't come to my house, not if you promised him free carrots and cabbage for a year."

"Well, if you do what I say, I reckon we'll get him there in two shakes of a tail!" continued Brer Wolf.

"How?" demanded Brer Fox suspiciously.

"You go home straight away and get into bed and act like you're dead, very, very dead. Now don't you make one sound until Brer Rabbit comes round to pay his respects to the dear departed. While he's standing over you pretending to mind that you've died, grab him and pop him in the pot on the fire. Cousin Fox, remember to have the water all ready and boiling. Brer Rabbit won't know what's hit him!" ended Brer Wolf.

"Great!" cried Brer Fox. "Then we can have rabbit stew and no more Brer Rabbit to torment us. Cousin Wolf, you are a genius."

So, Brer Fox raced home to pretend to be dead and Brer Wolf raced off to Brer Rabbit's house to tell him the sad news.

When Brer Wolf got there he knocked hard on the door, BANG, BANG. There was no reply. Brer Wolf began to shout, "Brer Rabbit, this is Brer Wolf. Come on out. I've got something mighty important to tell you."

From inside, Brer Rabbit replied, "I'm not

interested. I'm trying to sleep. Go away, Brer Wolf!"

"I've got bad news, Brer Rabbit. I wanted you to be the first to hear it, but I'll go and tell Brer Turtle instead."

"No!" yelled Brer Rabbit. "If it's bad news I want to be the first to know," and he opened the door and put out one eye and one ear.

"So what's this bad news, then?"

A tear ran down Brer Wolf's face.

"Brer Fox died this morning," he said mournfully and got out his large red spotted handkerchief.

"Really?" said Brer Rabbit suspiciously.

"Really, Brer Rabbit. My poor cousin never recovered from the time you dropped a brick on his head… never was his own self after that. Well, I'll be on my way. I just thought you would want to know, given that you and dear dead Cousin Fox had known each other for so long."

Brer Rabbit tried not to smile.

"This is very sad news you bring, Brer Wolf, and I want to thank you for letting me be the very first to hear it. As you say, Brer Fox and I go back a very long way."

"Least I could do, Brer Rabbit," wept Brer Wolf. "Now I must go and organise poor Cousin Fox's funeral."

No sooner had Brer Wolf gone than Brer Rabbit raced out of his house and round to Brer Fox's house.

"I want to see Brer Fox stone dead for myself," grinned Brer Rabbit.

When he got to the house, he pushed open the downstairs window and looked around. There was not a sound to be heard and there, lying on the bed, was Brer Fox in his Sunday best and with his hands folded across his chest.

"Poor Brer Fox," sniffed Brer Rabbit, and then more loudly, "he certainly is dead. Well, he looks dead. Mind you, I have always been told that when someone dies and a visitor comes to pay their last respects, dead people raise a leg in the air and shout 'Wahoo!'."

At that, Brer Fox raised one leg and shouted, "Wahoo!"

Half a second later, Brer Rabbit was off down

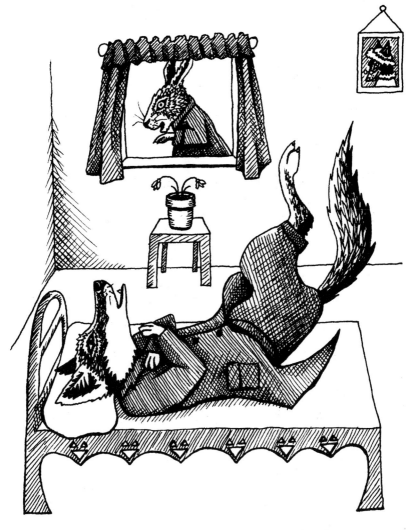

the road as far from Brer Fox's pot as his legs
would carry him.

"You can't fool me!" he shouted, as he ran
safely home.

ROMULUS AND REMUS

(BASED ON A ROMAN MYTH, ITALY)

Long ago by the banks of the river Tiber lived a king whom all his people loved called Numidor.

One day King Numidor's daughter, Princess Rhea, came to tell him that she was going to have a baby. Everyone was delighted and came to wish the princess well. Everyone, that is, except King Numidor's jealous brother Amulus, who was desperate to be king himself.

"If Princess Rhea's child turns out to be a boy," grumbled Amulus to himself, "that will secure the succession and I will never get a chance to be king. I must act quickly or all will be lost."

Late one night Amulus, and his men took over the palace and drove Numidor out into the neighbouring hills. Amulus made himself king. Princess Rhea begged Amulus to let her join her father.

"Certainly not, my dear," Amulus told her. "That would not be a good idea in your condition. Now, what kind of an uncle would I be if I sent you to live a rough life in the woods. You say Mars, the god of war, is the father of your child. Well, how would Mars feel about me if I let you go to your father in the woods when you might give birth at any moment?"

"If you don't let me go, Mars will punish you, Uncle," Rhea told him. "You were wrong to take my father's throne and I don't trust you. The child I am carrying will be revenged on you."

Later that night the princess gave birth to twin boys. As soon as he heard of it, Amulus ordered the boys to be brought to him. "You will never have my throne," he told the two screaming babies, "and you will never be revenged on me." Then he handed the newborn boys to his servant.

"Take these two screaming brats and throw them in the river and make sure you do it or it will be the worse for you."

The servant took the two babies and put them in a basket and, with tears in his eyes, pushed them into the river Tiber.

For a while, the basket floated down the river and then a slight wind came up and drove it onto the river bank. As night fell, the babies grew hungrier and hungrier and their screams got louder and louder.

A she-wolf, who had just given birth to cubs, was wandering along the river bank looking for food and heard the screams. When she found the two helpless human babies, she stood above them and let them drink her rich milk. The starving children sucked and sucked and the wolf let them drink until they were so full they fell asleep. All that night, the wolf kept watch over the sleeping babes and kept them warm and safe.

The next day Faustulus, a shepherd, came down to the river to get some water. The she-wolf howled to get his attention. Faustulus grabbed a stick and ran towards the river to drive the wolf away. Seeing that a human was coming who would find the little creatures she had worked so hard to keep alive, the wolf got ready to return to her own young ones. For one second her eyes caught those of Faustulus and then she disappeared into the forest.

Faustulus put down the stick when he heard the sound of children crying and, pulling aside the bushes, saw the two babies lying by the river.

A smile spread over the old shepherd's face.

"What fine, bonny boys," he cried. "Just what my wife and I need now that all our children are grown up and gone from home. Come on, my lovelies. Old Faustulus will look after you." Taking off his warm sheepskin jacket, the shepherd wrapped up the babes

and took them home as fast as he could manage.

"Look what I found by the river," he cried, as he flung open the door of his hut.

The shepherd's wife had a kind heart like her husband.

"The gods have sent them to us to care for," she cried. "You go and milk the goat. They'll be needing some milk. I'll lay them by the fire to keep warm."

"They're going to be tough those two," Faustulus told her. "They were cared for by a she-wolf. She must have fed them and kept them warm overnight. Then she made sure I found them before she ran off. They're not going to be ordinary, those two, you mark my words."

Faustulus and his wife called their adopted sons, Romulus and Remus, and like their true father, Mars the god of war, they grew up to be big and strong and wild.

One night, Faustulus came home with big cuts on his head and bleeding badly.

"What happened, Father?" asked Romulus.

"Some robbers set on me and stole two sheep," the shepherd told them. "I tried to stop them, but there were too many of them for me."

"We'll sort them out, don't you worry, Father. We'll get your sheep back, won't we, Romulus?" cried Remus.

"No doubt about it," agreed Romulus grimly and he picked up a big stick. "Come on, Remus. They can't have gone far."

The two brothers found the gang of robbers feasting on one of the stolen sheep and dividing up money and jewels that they had stolen. Waiting until it was very dark and the robbers were very drunk, the brothers crept into the camp and killed the thieves. They took the robbers' loot and returned to Faustulus's hut.

"Didn't I tell you these two would be tough?" chuckled Faustulus to his wife. Then turning to the young men, he said, "You two were fed by a she-wolf. You've got the power of a wolf pack in you. That's something really special."

"Father, here is the robbers' loot. It's for you."

"No," cried Faustulus. "To take it would make us as bad as the robbers. Share it out among the poor shepherds in the hills. Do something to make their hard lives better."

Not long after, another band of robbers started to rob and pillage in the area and once again Romulus and Remus went to sort them out. This time, they saw that the robbers had taken an old man prisoner and had tied him up and were making fun of him. As soon as it was dark, they rescued the old man and took him back to Faustulus

Faustulus and the old man talked deep into the night and the old man revealed that he was none other than King Numidor!

"The worst thing of all is that when my poor daughter Rhea gave birth to fine twin boys," he told his hosts, "my wicked brother Amulus took them away and had them thrown into the Tiber before they were a day old."

"When was this?" asked Faustulus, holding his breath.

"It must be eighteen years ago now," said Numidor sadly.

"Meet your grandsons!" cried Faustulus. "I found them by the river in a basket. They were saved by a she-wolf."

"A she-wolf!" exclaimed Numidor. "No wonder they are so big and strong. Come, my grandsons, embrace your grandfather who never expected to be happy again. You must come with me and meet your mother. What a wonderful day for all of us!"

To revenge Amulus, Romulus and Remus gathered together a large band of shepherds and drove the pretender from the palace and made Numidor king again.

"You must live here in the palace with your mother and me," cried Numidor. "You don't need to be shepherds any longer or fight robbers. Stay here and be my heirs."

"No, Grandfather," said the twins. "We are off to found our own cities for we were suckled by a she-wolf and can achieve great things."

The twin brothers each began to build a new city on the opposite banks of the river Tiber.

Romulus's city stretched across seven hills and he began to build a wall round his city to protect it. Remus crossed the river to visit his twin.

"What's that you're building, brother?" he asked.

"This is the beginning of the wall that will protect my city of the seven hills," replied Romulus proudly.

Remus looked at the wall that barely came up to his knees and roared with laughter.

"A wall to protect your city. You must be joking!" he jeered. "Look, I can jump over it easily. Do you really think your enemies will be scared silly by this little wall?"

"I worked very hard to build that wall, brother. These things take time and I don't need your sneering comments," Romulus said angrily. "So just be quiet!"

"But I like your sweet little wall," said Remus laughing. "It's a great little wall for jumping over.

You could hold the low-wall jumping Olympic contest here."

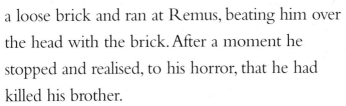

Romulus went red with rage. He picked up a loose brick and ran at Remus, beating him over the head with the brick. After a moment he stopped and realised, to his horror, that he had killed his brother.

As he wept over his twin's body, Romulus howled, "This is the wolf blood in me. Now I must learn to control it and I must build a great city and try to be a just and kind ruler like my grandfather. My poor brother Remus, how I will miss him. My city will be his memorial and I will make it a truly great place."

The city of Romulus became Rome and was the largest and most famous city of the Ancient World. Today, the symbol of Rome is the she-wolf feeding the two baby boys and there are statues in Rome of the event that led to the founding of the city.

MR WOLF AND HIS TAIL

(MEXICO)

Mr Wolf was padding round the open plains of Mexico when suddenly four huge and fierce dogs began to chase him. Mr Wolf began to run for his life.

"I've had it," he said to himself, as he began to slow down with exhaustion. Suddenly, he saw a cave up ahead, just large enough for him to get into, but too small for the dogs.

"What a piece of luck!" cried Mr Wolf, and he ran into the cave and lay on the cool earth floor and panted. After a minute, he looked round and saw in one corner a pool of water and in another a dead sheep.

"Food and drink! Perfect, I can stay here forever," cried Mr Wolf. "What a very clever wolf I am to have found this cave."

After eating and drinking, Mr Wolf listened to the dogs howling outside the cave. Suddenly, he addressed his four feet.

"Feet, feet!" he cried. "What did you do to help me find this fine safe cave?"

"We ran as fast as we could to bring you here and escape from the dogs," the feet replied.

"That is true," said the wolf. "You are very good feet and I thank you."

"And what did you do in my hour of need?" Mr Wolf demanded of his two ears.

"We listened very hard to find out which direction the dogs were coming from and helped you find the right way to go."

"That is true," agreed the wolf. "You are very fine ears and I thank you."

Then Mr Wolf asked his two eyes, "What did you do to help me when I was in such great danger?"

"We found you this wonderful safe cave," the eyes told him.

"That is indeed true," nodded Mr Wolf. "You are excellent eyes and I thank you. What a fine fellow I am to have such splendid feet and ears and eyes. I really am a prince among wolves."

Just then, he noticed his tail trailing in the dust.

"Oh, I forgot you," said Mr Wolf. "You, tail, how did you help when the dogs were on my trail? Nothing, that's what! You hung onto me and weighed me down so that the dogs nearly caught me. Now isn't that right?"

The tail got very angry because he had worked very hard to help the wolf keep his balance as he ran from the dogs, so he replied, "I did more than that. I waved to the dogs to tell them to hurry up and catch you!"

"Tail, you are horrible and I hate you," shouted Mr Wolf, and he bit his tail as hard as he could.

Then he cried out angrily, "You can go out of here this very minute. I don't want you here and neither do my four fast feet, or my two good eyes or my two sharp ears. Get out of here right now."

With that, he pushed his tail out of the cave. Of course, the four waiting dogs grabbed the tail and pulled Mr Wolf out of his safe cave and made him their prisoner. Too late, Mr Wolf realised how foolish and unfair he had been.